KRISTY KELLY

Finding Forgiveness

First published by Kristy Kelly 2019

Third edition

This book was professionally typeset on Reedsy.
Find out more at reedsy.com

Contents

Finding Forgiveness

Kristy Kelly

Dedication

This book is dedicated to the reviewer who reminded me of the importance of attention to detail.

Writing has always been a comfort to me, and I couldn't do it without the support of the friends and family I have in my life. I'm grateful to all of them.

Finally, this book is dedicated to you, dear reader. Thank you for letting me entertain you with the characters that dwell inside my mind. I hope they bring you as much joy as they bring me.

Chapter One

Kimberly

The perfect fall sky couldn't erase the sense of impending doom that loomed over her life. The last of her three children, Megan, bounced between the house and the storage truck, her excitement palpable. Had Kimberly ever been so young, or faced life with such anticipation? At fifty-two, nothing in her life brought the joy etched in her daughter's smile. Megan carried the last suitcase into the rented truck. The car they'd bought her when she graduated bore painted well wishes from her friends. Kimberly held back tears as she walked toward her daughter to say their last goodbye before Megan drove off to college. Though she was only going across the state, it might as well have been light-years away.

The sensation of loneliness crept in like a shadow behind her smile. It was something Kimberly had never really allowed herself to acknowledge—how empty their house had started to feel, long before Megan's departure. The manicured lawn crunched beneath her pumps, the lilies she'd nurtured for years now only deepened her pain. She blinked back the tears that threatened to fall. Her chest ached with each heartbeat that drove her closer to the end of life as she knew it.

It broke her to know she was no longer needed to care for her children. They still needed her love, she knew that, but it was different when they were on their own. When she hugged her youngest daughter, she let her tears fall. Though Megan promised to be home for Christmas, the holiday seemed light-years away instead of right around the corner. *But then, Kimberly thought, would Christmas matter when the man who had once been her world would not even be there?*

"Mom," Megan said as she shook her head and frowned. "I'm not leaving forever, you know."

Kimberly couldn't bring herself to speak, but nodded her agreement, wrapping her arms tightly around the youthful woman who shouldn't be old enough to drive off across the state.

"Also, the last time I did laundry, I turned everything pink. I'm sure that means you'll see me once a week," Megan added. Kimberly smiled. It was true. Megan struggled with the basics of adulthood, but Kimberly had worked hard to ensure her children had the tools to survive whatever life threw at them. It seemed like only yesterday Gregory had taught Megan how to ride her bike by the curb where they stood.

"Text me the moment you get there," Kimberly said, her head buried in Megan's dark tresses.

"I will, I promise," Megan said with a laugh, the excitement of her adventure shining in her bright eyes.

Gregory stepped out of the front door, arms loaded with boxes. Kimberly took a moment to admire his physique. Even at fifty-four, he was gorgeous. His black hair, sprinkled with white, made him look distinguished. The body he treated with care hadn't given in to the battle of age. His face, partly hidden by the mountain of boxes, had gone unshaven that morning, a patchwork of black and gray stubble lining his chin. She'd kissed that chin a thousand times, but as she stared, her mood darkened. *Her eyes lingered for just a moment too long. It was always the little things—the stubble, the line between his brows when he was irritated—that made her wonder how much she still loved him, or how much of her love had been lost to what he'd done.*

After Megan and Gregory said their goodbyes, Kimberly stepped onto the sidewalk that led to the front door. She waved as her daughter climbed into the moving truck. Megan waved back and blew a kiss to her father. Through teary eyes, Kimberly watched her daughter drive away.

Gregory put his arm around Kimberly's waist and watched the truck disappear in the distance. He winked at her. "Well, after almost thirty years of marriage, we're on our own." His deep voice sent a shiver down her spine, a familiar thrill she'd always felt when he spoke. She glanced at him. Despite the betrayal, she loved him with all her heart.

"In more ways than one." She slipped out of his arm and walked into the house. She went straight to their bedroom, wishing, once again, that they had separate rooms. As much as she sometimes hated him, he never failed to make her want him.

But that desire had dulled. The weight of his lies and betrayal had seeped into every part of their marriage. Still, the anger wasn't enough to quench the ache in her heart, the ache that came with the betrayal that left her feeling hollow.

He followed her. She glanced at him, straightening her spine, preparing to say what needed to be said. The serenity of their bedroom, decorated in their shared love of the outdoors, offered a sense of calm she needed to find her courage.

"What was that remark about?" His voice carried irritation. Gregory preferred things out in the open. He hated hidden meanings and riddles. Funny, considering the life he'd hidden from her.

"It means we'll be on our own. It means you'll be on your own in this house, and I'll be on my own at the hotel I'm moving into today."

She watched his face as the words sank in. His face reddened, the vein in his forehead pulsing. His dark brown eyes almost black, fixed on her.

"And to what do I owe the dishonor of my wife leaving me?" His voice was harsh, and Kimberly felt a pang in her chest. The pain in his voice made her want to retract her words for a moment.

"For two years, I've watched you lie in bed with another woman, all while I tortured myself hoping you'd change," she spat, the anger building as she spoke. "That made me realize I was worth nothing in your eyes. I promised myself that when the children left, I would too. Megan was the last, and she left today." With that, she turned toward the suitcase she'd packed earlier that morning.

"What are you talking about? I've never—this isn't what you think!" His voice was trembling, a mix of confusion and denial.

Kimberly's heart clenched, but she pushed on. "I hoped it was a phase, a mid-life crisis. She kept calling, telling me where you were when you said you were on a business trip."

Gregory moved toward her, but she stepped away.

"I changed my number, but the calls kept coming. Three months ago, I made the decision. I'd had enough." Kimberly's voice cracked as tears threatened to fall. "The children have left, and now, so have I."

Gregory's face was open with shock, his mouth hanging agape. "How could you not come to me? Did you have so little faith in me, in us, to believe a lie? Kimberly, look at me."

She stepped away, every step more painful than the last. "I can't. Goodbye, Gregory."

She fumbled with the doorknob, tears burning her eyes. She took a breath before she walked out of the room, not giving him the satisfaction of a final glance.

***

Gregory

After his wife walked away, his mind went to the day he proposed. The memory of that day gripped him with a force he couldn't shake, even as he tried to push it away. It was the summer he turned twenty-one, those last days of warmth before the chill of fall. Gregory climbed the steps to Kimberly's porch, knowing he'd be there for his usual Friday visit—three hours he cherished. In summers past, they'd allowed him only thirty minutes with her, but that wasn't enough. He wanted more. He wanted every hour, every moment, for the rest of his life.

His father's investment in his education had secured his future, but there was one thing missing—the fiery redhead who'd cast a spell on him from the moment he'd agreed to a double date. She was everything.

He knocked, and her father, Mr. Kilbane, answered. Gregory felt a strange sense of relief. Mr. Kilbane was easy to deal with—unlike Mrs. Kilbane, whose presence always intimidated him.

"Fall's coming," Mr. Kilbane said, stepping onto the porch with Gregory and closing the door behind him. The older man's silver hair curled at his ears, and the lines around his eyes and mouth spoke of a life well-lived, one filled with laughter. Gregory silently hoped to fare as well in his old age.

"Yes, sir," Gregory replied, his voice steady.

"You'll be heading back to school soon, I imagine." The elder Kilbane motioned toward the two Adirondack chairs on the front porch, an invitation to sit.

"Yes, sir, I got accepted to law school," Gregory answered as he sat down. His mouth went dry, nerves creeping in despite his preparations. He had rehearsed his speech, but now, with the moment at hand, the words caught in his throat.

"What are your intentions toward my daughter?" Mr. Kilbane's blunt question startled him. Usually, Kimberly's mother asked such direct questions; her father had always been more reserved. But now, the weight of Mr. Kilbane's gaze was unmistakable.

Gregory froze. A future without Kimberly wasn't a future he could imagine. It wasn't a decision—it was a certainty.

"I'll marry her, if she'll have me," he said, swallowing hard. "With your permission."

The quiet chuckle that followed surprised him. "Does she know that?"

The screen door slammed behind them, followed by the swift approach of a woman whose anger was as obvious as her beauty. Gregory's heart lurched. Kimberly. Her cheeks flushed, her face a mix of annoyance and something else he couldn't place. She wore her Sunday dress, the one she reserved for special occasions. Red curls cascaded down her back, and a bow rested in her hair. Even in frustration, she was breathtaking.

"How dare you tell my father we're getting married without asking me first?" she demanded, marching toward him and poking a finger into his chest.

"Well, I would've asked you, but I wanted your father's permission first,"

Gregory replied, biting the inside of his cheek to hide the laugh threatening to bubble up. Kimberly was angry—yes—but she was so damn adorable, her chest rising and falling with each breath.

"I'm not a child, Gregory. You ask me first." With that, she spun on her heel and stormed off the porch.

Gregory stared after her, lips pressed together to stop the laughter that threatened to escape. No one else had the power to make him laugh like she did. He was sure of one thing—he'd spend the rest of his life convincing her he was worthy of her. He would build a law firm that would provide for them, support them, ensure their happiness for decades to come. Nothing would stand in his way.

Her father, barely containing his own amusement, offered advice. "Go after her, or she'll only get worse. And make sure it's a church wedding."

Gregory gave a small smile, "Yes, sir." He bounded off the porch to catch up with Kimberly.

She stood near the edge of the yard, her blue dress swirling in the breeze, her arms crossed tightly. The fierceness in her posture reminded him of a warrior—small but determined. The look on her face was more comical than intimidating, like a kitten trying to challenge a Great Dane. He couldn't suppress the laughter any longer, his shoulders shaking as a deep chuckle escaped him.

"Don't you laugh at me, Gregory Davenport! I'm angry with you!" she snapped, but there was something in her eyes that told a different story.

"Marry me," he said, pulling out the ring he'd spent months saving for. It wasn't much, but it was perfect—he had enlisted his mother's help to pick it out, making sure it was the right symbol of his love.

"No," she pouted, making his heart race.

"Marry me, Kimberly."

"No." She raised an eyebrow, a smirk tugging at her lips.

"Kimberly Kilbane, marry me. Be the mother of my children, my partner in life, the woman I grow old with." Dropping to one knee, he held the ring up to her.

She froze, her hand flying to her mouth, as if the moment shocked her.

Panic seized Gregory's chest. Was she going to say no? His entire world felt like it was hanging in the balance.

"Say something," he urged, his voice shaky.

"Don't be dumb. You know I'll marry you. Mother and I have already finished my wedding dress."

He blinked, shocked. "How did you know? I didn't even know until recently."

"Gregory, you've been in love with me since you spilled ice cream on my dress at the state fair. I knew you'd figure it out eventually."

He shook his head, marveling at her. "You already knew? Why did you get angry with me then?"

"Because I didn't want you to propose in front of my dad. I wanted it to be special—just between us." She motioned around them, then chuckled, clearly amused by the whole thing.

He laughed too, relieved and overwhelmed by how much he loved her. She had manipulated the moment to get the proposal she wanted, but it didn't matter. She was perfect.

"In case you're wondering," Kimberly said, stepping closer and pulling him into her arms, "I love you, too." Her lips found his, sealing their engagement with a kiss.

The memory of that kiss now felt like a lifetime ago. Gregory's chest tightened as the pain of losing her hit him. He sank to the floor, unable to stop the tears from streaming down his face. She had walked out, believing a lie—a lie he couldn't understand.

Why had she believed that? Why had she thought he cheated on her? She hadn't given him a chance to explain, to defend himself. And now she was gone.

Numb, Gregory found his way to his office. He collapsed into the leather chair Kimberly had bought him, his eyes falling on the desk she'd designed for him. Everywhere he looked, he saw her—her presence was everywhere.

How could she have believed that lie?

Chapter Two

Kimberly

The victory she fought for with her words didn't bring the satisfaction she had expected. Kimberly drove a block from their house before pulling over. Heat surged in her eyes, quickly turning into the sting of tears. The moment she turned the engine off, they came flooding out.

Kimberly buried her face against the steering wheel and sobbed. A scream built from the pit of her stomach. At first, she shoved her fist into her mouth, fighting the urge to let it out. But the scream surged again, and this time, she let it rip. She threw her head back, mouth open, howling in agony. The sound tore at her throat, raw and hoarse, until she could no longer summon the strength to keep going.

She cried for herself. She cried for her children. She cried for Gregory, too. At one point, he had loved her—he had to have, right?

Her thoughts spiraled, battling between the man she once knew and the man she had come to doubt. She had fought so hard to believe he could never do something like this to her. It wasn't in his nature. But the calls came. Relentless and insistent, slowly chipping away at her resolve, until doubt crept in. Then came the photograph. Every detail of it was seared into her memory—the way the stranger looked at him, her eyes filled with admiration. Kimberly didn't recognize her, but that look... the worship in her eyes as she gazed at her husband… it burned through her.

As the tears slowed, Kimberly glanced at herself in the rear-view mirror. Her eyes were red and swollen, her makeup ruined, mascara streaking down her cheeks. She inhaled deeply, wiped her face with the back of her hand, and started the car again, easing back onto the road.

By the time Kimberly pulled into the hotel parking lot, her nerves were shot. White knuckles gripped the steering wheel. She placed the car in park, then turned off the ignition. A strange numbness settled over her, as if her body was trying to detach from her emotions. She disconnected her cell phone from the car, shoving it into her purse without looking at it.

She knew she looked a mess—like a walking nightmare—but she had no strength to care. She entered the revolving door of the hotel. The soft Christmas music enveloped her, soothing the frantic pace of her mind. Warmth surrounded her, but it didn't reach inside.

A woman in a smart suit with large hoop earrings stared blankly at her as she approached the counter. Kimberly placed her overnight bag on the countertop, and her identification on top. Without saying anything more than the bare minimum, the woman handed her a box of tissues. Kimberly blinked back the fresh wave of tears threatening to fall, and took them gratefully.

The check-in process was quick, and soon she was handed the key to her room. She was already too tired to be anything but numb.

Once inside, Kimberly locked the door behind her. The silence pressed down on her, making the weight of her emotions feel even heavier. She reached for her phone and dialed her mother's number.

"Kilbane residence," came the familiar voice, unperturbed by technology despite her seventy-four years.

"Hello, Mama," Kimberly said softly.

"Hello, darling. I thought you'd call yesterday. How's Megan settling in? Are you lonely in that big house without her?" Her mother's concern hit Kimberly like a wave, threatening to pull her under. She struggled to keep her composure.

"Megan's fine. I didn't want to call right away and smother her." Guilt tugged at her. She hadn't thought of her children at all in the rush of everything else.

"Are you feeling okay?" Her mother's tone shifted to one of concern.

"I'm fine," Kimberly lied, forcing the words out. She couldn't bring herself to explain.

"You sound a little stuffy, though. You know Megan could never forget her mother. You're just tired, darling. There's no need for tears."

Kimberly's chest tightened. She blinked hard, fighting the tears. "Mama, I'm not crying because Megan left… I left Gregory."

The silence that followed seemed to stretch on forever, though it was only a minute.

"Please tell me you didn't leave him for the nonsense you were talking about a few years ago," her mother said, the words laced with disbelief.

"I don't think Gregory cheating on me is 'nonsense,' Mama," Kimberly replied, her voice tinged with anger.

"Gregory cheating on you is nonsense," her mother retorted.

"I didn't want to believe it, either, but the calls never stopped. They knew where he was. They knew things I didn't." Kimberly's voice shook with the weight of it all.

"And what did Gregory say when you confronted him?"

"I never asked him," Kimberly admitted, the regret choking her words. "I trusted him too much. By the time I found out, it was too late."

"Sounds to me like you weren't faithful to him either," her mother said, her words slicing through Kimberly's heart.

"How can you say that?" Kimberly's anger flared. "I was faithful to him!"

"You don't understand, Kimberly," her mother said gently. "Being faithful isn't just about not sleeping with someone else. It's about trusting them beyond what you hear, beyond the doubt."

"Mama, why, when I need you the most, are you defending him?" Kimberly's voice cracked as she struggled to understand why her mother wasn't supporting her. She refused to hear the truth in her words.

"There are no sides when a marriage breaks apart, darling. There are only two people left to rebuild what's been destroyed."

Kimberly swallowed hard, her heart breaking. She couldn't face the weight of her mother's words, the truth she wasn't ready to accept. "I have to go, Mama. I'll call you soon."

"Remember the promise you made on your wedding day, Kimberly. Trust in God to help you through this. Pray for Gregory and pray for yourself."

The sternness of her mother's voice echoed in her mind, the same as it had on her wedding day.

"Yes, Mama. Goodbye." Kimberly ended the call, but her mother's words lingered in her mind.

The memory of her wedding vows flashed before her eyes:

"Do you take Gregory as your lawful husband, to have and to hold, for better or for worse, for richer or for poorer, in sickness and in health, to love and to cherish, until death do you part?"

"I did my part," Kimberly whispered aloud. "I loved him. I cherished him."

"I take this ring as a sign of my love and faithfulness, in the name of the Father, the Son, and the Holy Spirit." Her voice, once so sure and full of hope, now felt hollow.

"I was faithful to him!" she yelled, her voice echoing through the empty hotel room.

Her mother's words echoed in her head: "Faithfulness means trusting them beyond anything you hear, no matter what."

Kimberly slammed the door behind her and began pacing the room. She had done the right thing. She had no choice. He had given her none.

"Why didn't I just ask him? Why didn't I confront him sooner?" Her thoughts spiraled out of control.

She kept hitting the same wall, the same question: What kind of person spends years destroying her own marriage?

The calls had never revealed the other woman's identity, but Kimberly had always suspected it was a mistress. She couldn't help but sympathize with the woman. After all, Kimberly knew what it was like to love a man and share him with someone else.

Even now, part of her wanted Gregory to come looking for her, to drive to every hotel in town, begging her to come home. She wanted him to promise that everything he'd done was over, and that life without her was impossible.

Was that too much to ask? A faithful husband? She loved him. She deserved his loyalty and respect. She deserved his undivided love.

Kimberly collapsed onto the bed, curling into a fetal position. Tears fell again, soaking into the pillow as her heart broke once more.

***

Gregory

Unable to contain his restlessness, Gregory called the one man he knew would help him win his wife back: his lifelong best friend and partner at the law firm they owned, Michael. Michael had been the best man at Gregory's wedding and was the godfather to all three of his children.

When Michael's wife, Angelica, answered the phone, Gregory groaned inwardly. He'd never understood why Michael had married such a disagreeable woman. She shouted for her husband, and soon Michael came on the line.

"Gregory, is everything all right? Kimberly's not having a meltdown now that the last kid's left, is she?" The concern in Michael's voice sent a sharp pang through Gregory's chest. The bitterness toward his wife simmered as he recounted what had happened.

"I'll be there in ten minutes," Michael said after listening, as if sensing that Gregory needed someone to listen more than to advise.

True to his word, Michael knocked on Gregory's door exactly ten minutes later. Familiar with the house from their vacations, he punched in the code and entered when Gregory called out for him to come in. Gregory remained at his desk, his gaze fixed on the surface as Michael entered the den and helped himself to a glass of bourbon. He looked at Gregory, his face a mixture of confusion and concern. "What did you do?"

Gregory wasn't sure if Michael was asking about what he'd done to cause the situation or what he'd done afterward.

"She thinks I was having an affair—or even two, apparently, for a long time now." The bile rose in his throat as he spoke. Each word stoked his anger further. How dare Kimberly accuse him without giving him a chance to defend himself?

"Were you?" Michael's voice was devoid of emotion.

As the question sank in, Gregory's anger surged. He leapt from his chair, stormed around the desk, and swung a fist that connected squarely with Michael's chin. Pain shot through his knuckles from the impact.

"I guess that answers my question," Michael said, unruffled, smiling slightly as he rubbed his chin and placed a steadying hand on Gregory's shoulder.

"What are you thinking, Mike? I would never cheat on Kimberly. I love her, and the fact that she believes I'd do something like that—it kills me." Gregory sank back into his chair, exhausted by the day's events.

"What are you going to do?" Michael asked, never one to waste time with trivial questions. He got straight to the core of any problem, a trait that had helped make their firm so successful. Michael could fix anything.

"I figure I have a few options. One would be to kill her for putting me through this," Gregory said, grinning darkly. "Two would be to hunt down whoever filled her head with these lies and kill them. And three, to fight for her—to make her see how wrong she is."

Michael regarded him with an unreadable expression, his face briefly expressionless. The red mark on his chin reminded Gregory of the emotional rollercoaster he was on.

"Well, first things first," Michael said at last, "we need to figure out what made Kimberly think you were unfaithful." With that, Michael dove right into plotting a solution.

Gregory felt grateful to have such a supportive friend, an ally in the fight to save his marriage. He could only hope the spirit of Christmas might open Kimberly's heart enough for a miracle.

Long after Michael left the den, Gregory wandered into the kitchen, gazing at the spotless surfaces. His wife had even cleaned the kitchen before leaving him. The thought lingered in his mind as he paced the empty house. Suddenly, the phone rang, pulling him back. On his way to answer it, he tripped over one of Megan's swimming trophies. He sucked in a breath, resisting the urge to curse. He picked up the receiver with a sigh, his voice barely audible.

"Hello?"

A woman's voice came on the line. "Mrs. Davenport, he's with her again. He bought her a teddy. Check his credit card statements. Why do you stay with a man who flaunts his affairs right in your face?" The line went dead before he could respond. The caller had clearly mistaken him for Kimberly.

Gregory stared at the phone, stunned. He knew he should have been out tonight—Kimberly would have been the one to receive that call. Replaying the words in his mind, he remembered buying a teddy earlier, but it hadn't been for a mistress or even for Kimberly. He'd picked it up as a gag gift for Allen in accounting, who'd recently finished his studies to become a pastor. The bright red teddy was meant to be a funny reminder of what Allen was "giving up."

"Son of a…" Gregory began, but the phone rang again. He let it ring four times until his daughter's voice came on the answering machine. He couldn't bring himself to speak to his children just yet. He had to figure out what was going on. The woman's voice from the phone call continued to haunt him. He knew he'd heard it before.

When Michael didn't respond to his shouted calls, Gregory picked up his cell and dialed his friend.

"Careful, Gregory," Michael answered dryly. "You're calling more than a teenage girl."

"I just got a call from our mystery woman. She told Kimberly that the teddy I bought today was for my mistress," Gregory said, unable to keep the disgust from his voice.

"Well, that's our first real clue. Give me twenty minutes, and make sure your fax machine is on." Michael hung up without another word.

Michael returned half an hour later, a satisfied grin on his face. "Phone records."

"I don't know why I didn't think of that myself," Gregory admitted.

"Because your first reaction was anger, your second was violence. Not much left over for rational thinking."

"Are you sure this is legal?"

"You're pulling the phone records from your own line. And Jack won't mind—you did him a favor back in the day," Michael reassured him.

They sat together, watching the fax machine as it printed out the call log. Gregory was grateful Michael stayed by his side that evening, filling the silence Kimberly's absence left behind.

After the initial shock wore off, he began to see Kimberly's actions as a defection. She hadn't trusted him enough even to ask about the accusations; she'd simply taken the caller at their word. His goal was to shove proof of his innocence in her face, to make her understand what she'd put him through. Then, perhaps, he'd graciously take her back—after she groveled a bit.

The fax emitted a series of beeps, and Gregory's heart lifted for the first time that evening. As soon as the last page printed, he snatched up the sheets and scanned the incoming call list.

"Well?" Michael prompted.

Gregory sighed, staring at the number listed right before his daughter's call. It had come from his office.

Now he had to decide what to do. He could march to the hotel where Kimberly was staying—he'd checked the charges on the joint credit card as soon as she left and knew her location. He could shove the phone records at her, as he'd planned. But the more he thought about it, the more he realized it would only escalate the situation.

Someone had poisoned Kimberly against him, feeding her lies until her heart had turned. He wanted to believe she'd struggled to accept it at first, that she hadn't mentioned it because she didn't fully believe it.

Though he felt betrayed, he still loved her as deeply as the day he married her.

His phone rang, interrupting his thoughts. Grace's number flashed on the caller ID. He groaned, knowing that if he didn't answer, she'd come storming over to find out what was going on.

"Hello, my angel," Gregory said.

"Hi, Daddy. I was calling to check on Mama. I thought she might need some moral support now that the last chick has flown the coop."

Gregory closed his eyes, debating how to respond.

"She's so inconsolable that she took the AmEx to Pittsburgh," he said finally. "She mentioned something about presents." It wasn't a complete lie—she had taken the AmEx, and she had mentioned Christmas shopping.

"Oh, retail therapy at its finest. Why didn't you go?"

"Someone has to work to pay off that AmEx bill."

"Ah, work—your mistress." Grace laughed.

Her words hit him hard. She was right, in a way. Work *had* been his mistress, but not in the way she thought. He'd cheated on Kimberly emotionally by prioritizing his job over their relationship.

"Look, Daddy, I have to go. Give Mama my love," Grace said, hanging up before he could reply.

Gregory stared at the phone, guilt flooding him. If he'd been more attentive, more focused on his marriage, Kimberly might not have been so easily swayed by lies. He wouldn't have let the distance between them grow.

He'd courted her with passion once, and it wasn't too late to do it again. Determined, he crumpled the phone records and threw them into the wastebasket.

Gregory smiled to himself. What better way to prove his love than to win her heart all over again?

Chapter Three

Kimberly

Kimberly needed fresh air. She stepped out of her hotel room, determined to find some space away from the tangled mess in her mind. She walked down to the lobby, hoping a quiet stroll in the park would clear her head. As she approached the front door, a voice called her name from behind. She turned to see a man standing at the desk, holding a single rose in his hand.

Confused, she walked back toward him. "I'm Kimberly Davenport."

"This is for you, ma'am." He offered her the rose, his hand outstretched. Kimberly took it, staring at the brilliant flower in wonder. The delicate petals glowed with life, and for a brief moment, it distracted her from the chaos of her thoughts.

Her eyes scanned the rose for a card. It was attached to the stem. She opened it and read the words, feeling a lump form in her throat:

There weren't enough roses in the shop for each day that I took you for granted. So, I bought all they had.

It was unsigned. Her heart sank. Gregory knew how much she loved roses. This wasn't a gesture of love—it was emotional blackmail.

The deliveryman cleared his throat, drawing her attention back. "There's more in the truck. Where would you like them?"

"More?" Kimberly could barely hide her disbelief.

"Yeah. A lot more. Not a big market for roses in December, so I had to get them from a couple different suppliers." He smiled, clearly unaware of the storm brewing inside her.

Kimberly's anger surged, but she fought to stay composed. She followed the man outside to his truck, still clutching the single rose. When he opened the back, she gasped. The entire space was lined with roses—red, white, pink, yellow—all of them perfect and breathtaking.

Her pulse quickened. Gregory had bought every single rose in the shop, just as his note had said.

"Could you send them to my house?" she asked, trying to sound calm despite the storm inside her.

"Sure, I can do that. These are the last roses, so I won't be delivering any more today." He grinned and jotted down her address, seeming oblivious to the emotional havoc he was causing.

Kimberly handed him the rose. She needed time to think, time to process this absurdity. As she made her way back to her car, her irritation with Gregory grew. Roses didn't fix years of betrayal. They didn't erase the damage he'd done. She needed to confront him, but she wasn't ready to do that yet—not in the emotional chaos of the moment.

If anyone could help her sort through her emotions, it would be Father Rochelle. She called ahead to make sure he could see her before she returned to her hotel. The priest was always accessible to his parishioners, and today, she needed his guidance more than ever.

Arriving at the church, Kimberly slipped through the side entrance and made her way to Father Rochelle's office. She knocked softly before entering, grateful that he didn't hesitate when she asked to meet without an appointment.

"Kimberly, I'm glad you're here," Father Rochelle greeted her warmly. "Please, sit. You sounded upset on the phone. What's troubling you?"

She sank into the chair across from him, feeling the weight of her emotions pressing down on her. "Thank you for seeing me. I know you're busy with the Christmas services, but I really need your help."

"What's on your mind?"

Kimberly took a deep breath and began speaking, her words tumbling out in a rush. She told him everything—leaving Gregory, the call from the other woman, her confusion, and the overwhelming flood of emotions she couldn't seem to sort through. Father Rochelle listened patiently, only interrupting to ask a few clarifying questions.

By the time she finished, she was dabbing at her eyes with a tissue, feeling both relieved and more conflicted than ever.

"Oh, my child," Father Rochelle said softly, his voice filled with empathy. "I wish you had come to me sooner. The three of us could have worked through these issues together. But let me ask you this—are you certain, without any doubt in your heart, that Gregory has been unfaithful to you?"

The question hung in the air, heavy with implications. Kimberly hesitated. Her mind screamed the answer she thought she knew, but her heart wasn't so sure. She had never caught him, never seen it with her own eyes.

"No," she whispered, her voice barely audible.

Father Rochelle nodded. "Then there is still hope for you both. We will pray for guidance, and perhaps our Lord will grant you the clarity you seek."

He prayed for peace and understanding—for both Kimberly and Gregory—and by the time he finished, Kimberly's face was streaked with tears.

"Thank you, Father," she said, her voice trembling.

"I would like to see you both soon," he added.

"I'll talk to him. I'll tell him you'd like to meet."

"Be strong, Kimberly. Trust in God to guide you," Father Rochelle said, his voice steady and reassuring.

Kimberly nodded, wiping her eyes. She left the office feeling a strange mix of relief and uncertainty. Her heart was still heavy with the doubt she hadn't been able to shake.

As she drove back to the hotel, she replayed the priest's words over and over in her mind. She prayed for answers, for clarity—anything that would help her make sense of the mess she was in. But as soon as she arrived at the hotel, she realized she couldn't escape the storm raging inside her.

"Excuse me, my room card isn't working," Kimberly said as she approached the front desk. She'd tried it several times before giving up.

The woman behind the counter glanced at the card and then at the computer. "Mrs. Davenport, room 1201, the penthouse suite. The key isn't working?"

Kimberly frowned. "The penthouse? I'm not in the penthouse."

The woman checked again, her brow furrowing in confusion. "According to the system, we upgraded your room this morning. Same American Express card as the original reservation."

Gregory. Of course. She tried to keep her emotions in check. "Thank you for checking. I'll need a new key."

With the new key in hand, Kimberly grumbled her way up to the penthouse suite. She didn't know what Gregory was up to, but she was determined to confront him. When she opened the door to the suite, though, all her anger dissipated in an instant. The room was beyond luxurious—glistening marble floors, a stunning view of the city, and a king-sized bed covered in soft, inviting linens. It was a dream come true.

For someone else, she thought bitterly.

As she wandered through the suite, her heart ached with the realization that Gregory wouldn't be there to share it with her. That was the reason she was here—alone.

A knock at the door interrupted her thoughts. She wasn't expecting anyone, so she opened the door, only to find a bellhop with a cart laden with champagne, strawberries, and a chocolate fondue fountain.

"I didn't order this," Kimberly said, confused.

"We received the request on your behalf," the bellhop said, with an air of polite formality. "Your driver is waiting for you in the sitting room, and the concierge has arranged for a car to take you wherever you need to go."

"My driver?" Kimberly echoed, her mind racing.

"Yes, ma'am. A black stretch limo, with a uniformed driver, just as requested."

Gregory, again. She felt a knot form in her stomach. He was giving her the weekend she'd always dreamed of—without him.

"Thank you," she said softly. The bellhop left, but Kimberly's thoughts only grew more tangled. He had remembered the weekend she'd always wanted, but without him. It made her want him here, beside her, sharing this moment.

Her emotions warred inside her as she stared at the door. She didn't know whether to thank him or ask him to leave her alone.

Finally, she picked up the phone and dialed his office.

"Gregory Davenport," his voice answered, calm and warm.

"Hello, Gregory," she said, her heart pounding.

"I was hoping you'd call," he said, his voice tinged with relief.

"Why are you doing this?" Kimberly asked, frustration bubbling to the surface.

"Because you deserve this. I've failed you in the past, and I'm sorry. I'm trying to make up for it."

Kimberly didn't know what to say. She was caught between anger and longing. "Why now? I don't know what to think or feel. I can't decide if I'm angry at you for doing this, or grateful you remembered."

"I refuse to give up on us, Kimberly. I love you. I'd like to take you on a date—just one date. No pressure. You pick the time and place."

Her mind spun, but a part of her wanted to see what else he had planned. "Okay, one date."

"I'll meet you tomorrow at 7:00 p.m. at our favorite Italian place," he said, sounding thrilled.

"It's quite a distance from my hotel, but it seems I have a driver who will take me there. Goodbye, Gregory."

She hung up, feeling more confused than ever.

***

Gregory

A knock at the door jolted Gregory from his thoughts. He glanced through the peephole and saw a man standing with a crate full of roses. His stomach dropped. Kimberly hadn't kept the flowers, but it didn't surprise him—he'd overdone it, hadn't he? He'd gone for the grand gestures when small ones would've had more meaning. With a sigh, he opened the door.

"Yes?" Gregory asked, his voice heavy with fatigue.

The florist, a tall man with a professional smile, set the first crate down at Gregory's feet. He wasn't done. He placed another, then another, until the foyer was filled with a small mountain of crates.

"Ms. Davenport requested the delivery to the house," the man said, his tone formal, but with a hint of sympathy. He handed Gregory a clipboard.

"Mrs.," Gregory corrected, the word slipping out before he could stop it. He winced. It had been years since he had to make such a correction. But then again, Kimberly could've introduced herself as "Ms." for all he knew. The thought left a bitter taste in his mouth, but he pushed it aside.

"Sorry, Mrs. She did keep one, though. The one with the card," the florist added, his expression shifting to something more hopeful.

Twelve crates. A dozen full of roses. Gregory stared at them, feeling both guilt and a flicker of hope. She kept one. She could've discarded them all, trampled them underfoot like she had with their marriage. But one? That was something. Maybe she hadn't entirely given up on him yet.

He turned back to the florist, trying not to show how the gesture, once meant to capture Kimberly's attention, was already starting to feel like a misstep. "Thank you. I'll handle the rest." He signed the clipboard absently, his thoughts already elsewhere.

As the florist left, Gregory felt the weight of the roses pressing down on him. The over-the-top gesture, meant to show his love, now felt like a mistake. Kimberly was never one for grand gestures. She preferred simplicity—small vacations, quiet moments. He had heard her talk about those things for years, but somehow, work always got in the way. He'd planned lavish trips, but each time, his obligations pulled him away. Now, those missed moments echoed in his mind, like failures he couldn't undo.

He remembered one time saying, "Let's go, just the two of us. We'll spend the weekend in the penthouse, strawberries, champagne. Chauffeur service. It'll be fun."

But she never wanted that. She preferred quiet time. He had always been too caught up in business. She had stopped mentioning her dreams of small getaways long ago, and he'd let it slide. What had he given her in return for everything she did for him, for their family? A paycheck and the occasional romantic gesture. Not nearly enough.

His thoughts wandered back to their biggest fights—those about family vacations. Kimberly always made it a point to take the kids on their annual camping trips. She called it their reset week. The kids hated it at first—no technology, no screens—but by the end, they loved it. Gregory had planned to join them every year, but work always came first. And Kimberly was always there, holding everything together. He had failed her so many times.

He thought of his most recent failure. Kimberly had stepped up in ways he never could. She had raised their children, managed the house. And he… he had given her a paycheck.

The realization was painful but undeniable. He had been a neglectful husband, taking advantage of a woman who had given him everything.

The first step to solving any problem was admitting it. And Gregory was certain—he had failed his wife. But it wasn't too late to fix it.

He picked up the phone and made a few quick calls. It didn't take much to arrange an upgrade to Kimberly's hotel room, or to book a stretch limousine to drive her around town for the week. Strawberries, champagne, chocolate fondue. It wasn't much, but it was something. He would show her how much he needed her—how much he had taken her for granted.

But why had it taken him this long to realize it?

His mind churned with the question, and with the uncomfortable realization that he had been too focused on his career and neglected the one person who mattered most. And how had he not seen the lie Kimberly believed—the one about him and another woman? He couldn't understand how it had happened, but he knew that his neglect had made it too easy for her to believe.

He couldn't change the past, but he could make sure she knew he was fighting for her now.

With that resolve, the weight of the roses seemed to lift from his shoulders. He had spent the morning hoping the flowers would bring Kimberly running back to him. That hope had evaporated quickly. Now, he would focus on the next steps. Work was his only option for now. He couldn't risk his children finding out the truth too soon.

As for the person who had planted the seeds of doubt in Kimberly's mind—

Gregory was certain they worked in his office. That person was close. He didn't know who yet, but he would find them. He needed answers.

The phone call he had received from the mystery woman had come from one of the open lines in the building. Only three direct lines existed. The rest were extensions. Gregory was sure he could trace it back. It wouldn't be easy, but it was possible.

He considered installing a camera, but the logistics were tricky. If word got out, the culprit would know. Gregory didn't have the luxury of time. It was a risk he had to take. He'd enlist Michael to help him monitor the phone lines and set a trap. They would wait for the right moment.

But why? Why would anyone in his office want to hurt him like this? The betrayal felt personal. Someone who worked for him had deliberately set out to destroy his life.

Gregory stared at the intercom and pressed the button. "Emma, please bring me all the files on the employees we've hired in the last five years. Both current and former."

There was a slight pause before she responded. "Yes, sir."

He waited as Emma gathered the files. When she returned, she stacked them in front of him.

"Can I help with anything else?" she asked.

Emma had been his administrator for twenty years. Her loyalty was unquestionable, but Gregory couldn't involve her. Not in this.

"Thank you, Emma. You've been a great help. I'm not sure what I'm looking for yet, but I'll let you know if I need anything." He gave her a soft smile as he dismissed her.

Once Emma left, Gregory began sorting through the files. The task felt daunting, but he knew he had to find the reason behind the betrayal. Who would want to destroy Kimberly like this? And why?

The pile of involuntary terminations was small—a comfort to his pride. He started with the voluntary terminations, flipping through files and scrolling through social media. But there were no obvious red flags. Nothing stood out.

Next, he moved on to the involuntary terminations. His hope waned as he found no useful information. The current employees were next. He sifted through the files carefully, determined to find something—anything—that would explain what was happening. The person who poisoned Kimberly's mind needed to be found. And Gregory was determined to be the one to do it.

Chapter Four

Kimberly

Kimberly couldn't believe she'd agreed to this. People didn't date after a marriage had ended—especially when one of them had left. She shouldn't be here. Not yet. Not when her emotions were still raw, not when she still had so many unanswered questions. Just because Gregory thought this whole situation was a good idea didn't mean she had to follow suit. She had to remember why she left. The other woman. The mystery that had slowly poisoned their marriage. His lover, his mistress.

She stepped into the cool night air, the chill biting at her skin as she tugged the thin sweater tighter around her shoulders. The jeans she wore were more out of necessity than choice—she hadn't put much effort into her appearance. She just wanted tonight to be over. She would tell him once and for all that their marriage was finished. The lies, the deceit, the emotional turmoil—it all had to end. She couldn't live with a man who had no respect for her, not after everything he'd done.

The restaurant Gregory had chosen was a local favorite—one they'd frequented with his best friend, Michael, and his wife. The memories of them laughing together, of Gregory smiling at her as he uncorked a bottle of wine, hit her harder than she expected. Maybe this wasn't the best place to have this conversation. Maybe it was a mistake to come here at all.

But she had to go through with it. She had to do this.

Gathering her resolve, she stepped out of the limousine and walked toward the entrance. The clatter of voices and the warm glow of the restaurant's lights filled the air, a stark contrast to the cold weight in her chest. She'd come early, determined to take control of the situation. Tonight, it wasn't Gregory who would call the shots. She wanted him to hear her, really hear her, without his pride getting in the way.

When she spoke, she would be calm, rational. She would be the one who stood firm. The words she had prepared swirled in her mind, like a mantra. There would be no more lies. No more pretending. She would walk away, and maybe—just maybe—she could finally start to heal.

Her confidence faltered when she saw him. Gregory. Standing at the entrance, smiling like he always did. Just the sight of him made her heart do a little flip, a reminder of the affection that still lingered, even after everything. No matter how hard she tried, a part of her still loved him.

"Hello, darling," he said, his voice warm and affectionate as he leaned in to kiss her cheek before sitting across from her.

"Hi," she replied, her voice catching in her throat. She hated how easily he disarmed her, how his presence made her feel insecure when she should be strong. She had planned for this night, had convinced herself she was in control. But now, sitting across from him, all those carefully constructed walls started to crumble.

"You look nice," he said, his eyes lighting up with something Kimberly couldn't quite place.

"Thanks. We need to talk, Gregory. This… this has gone too far."

"I know. We need to make this right."

Their waiter arrived to take their drink order, and Kimberly chose water. Gregory ordered a soda, and she used the moment to gather her thoughts. She wasn't about to let him derail her. Not this time.

"I only have one question," she said, her voice steady.

"I was never unfaithful, Kimberly."

"That's your story, and you're sticking to it, huh?" she asked, her voice laced with disbelief as she shook her head.

"The truth doesn't change," he insisted. "You can ask today, or ten years from now, and my answer will remain the same. You are the only woman in my life."

"Why can't you just be honest with me?" she asked, her voice rising louder than she'd intended. She glanced around, realizing they weren't the only couple in the restaurant. But the heat of her frustration made it hard to care.

His face fell, a flicker of vulnerability that she wasn't sure she could trust. "I can see now that you came here with your mind already made up. What will it take for you to believe in the man you married, instead of the person who's supposedly out to destroy our relationship?"

"The truth," she replied, her voice cold, cutting through the air.

"Then let me get it," he insisted, his voice gaining intensity. "Let me find out who did this to us."

"That shouldn't be hard," she shot back, standing now, unable to sit at the same table as him for one more second. "You see him every morning in the mirror."

His face twisted in disbelief. "Kimberly, believe me, I never cheated on you."

"She knew about the scar you got from hopping the fence when you were twenty-two," Kimberly snapped. "The only two people who should know about that are me and your doctor. Every time I checked on you, I'd find out she was right."

"Kimberly, please—"

"No!" she interrupted, the anger she'd been holding back for so long spilling over. "I loved you with everything I had. And you destroyed something so pure, so right. All for what, Gregory? A quick fling because you were having a midlife crisis? I deserved better than that!"

"And I deserved the chance to defend myself," he said quietly, his voice filled with hurt.

His words felt like a slap. Kimberly's vision blurred with the heat of her emotions. "You had your chance. But you never came back to me. You never even tried. You just threw it all away for someone else!"

Unable to bear another moment in his presence, Kimberly turned and stormed out of the restaurant. The air outside felt colder, sharper, as she rushed to the waiting limousine. Thank God it was there—thank God she didn't have to stand around, waiting for him to come after her. But she knew he would. She could feel it in her bones, her whole being praying for him to follow her.

Back in her hotel room, she paced the floor like a caged animal, guilt clawing at her from every angle. She had meant to be strong, to stand firm. But now, with the anger fading and the weight of her words settling on her shoulders, she felt small. She had lashed out, unable to see past the bitterness that had been eating away at her for so long.

Gregory had only wanted to defend himself. And she had trampled on that. The grand gestures—his truckload of roses, the penthouse suite, the driver waiting for her—did he think they would buy her back? Could she not see the love behind them?

She knew better than that. She knew Gregory's gestures weren't about buying her forgiveness; they were about showing her how deeply he still cared. And she had ignored it, dismissed it all in her rush to push him away.

Before she could talk herself out of it, she grabbed the phone and dialed the number of the house. Her fingers trembled against the receiver.

"Hello?" His voice was thick, groggy. Had he been sleeping?

"Did I wake you?" she asked, her guilt rising like a tide.

"No," he said, his voice still thick with sleep. "Are you all right?" Even after everything she had put him through, his first concern was still for her.

"Gregory, I'm sorry," she said, the words tasting like ash on her tongue. "For how I behaved tonight. It was… juvenile. Uncalled for."

"Oh, Kimberly," he sighed, the weight of his own grief pressing through his words. "I just… I wish I could make this right. I miss you. I can't stand being apart."

"Can we just talk? Like we used to?" She could barely speak, the lump in her throat making her words tight and raw.

"Anything you want. We can talk about the weather, if you want. Just… please, let's talk." His voice cracked with the weight of his emotions.

Kimberly smiled through the tears that threatened to spill. "Okay. No heavy stuff. Let's just talk."

They talked about the small things—work, memories, the little moments they had once shared. No mention of the past week. No accusations. Just them, slipping into the easy camaraderie they once had. It felt comfortable, like they had never been apart. For a moment, it was just the two of them, finding solace in each other's company again.

"Remember the Ferris wheel?" Gregory asked, his voice filled with affection.

"How could I forget?" Kimberly replied, her heart aching as the memory washed over her.

She let herself drift back to that night, to the young girl she used to be, and to the man who had once made her believe in forever.

***

Gregory

The following morning, Gregory sat in the kitchen, a steaming cup of coffee in hand, his mind replaying the phone call with Kimberly. The words they'd exchanged echoed in his thoughts, keeping him awake most of the night.

"Well, I guess I should let you get some sleep. I'm glad you called," he had said. Though he didn't want the call to end, it had been well past midnight.

"We haven't stayed up late talking on the phone in more years than I care to count," she had replied, her voice carrying a soft smile. Another reminder of how he'd failed her. Kimberly had always been the one constant in his life, yet he had taken her for granted at every turn.

"I promised I'd keep the conversation light, and I will. So, I'll end the call with 'I love you,' and I hope you have pleasant dreams."

"Thank you for keeping your promise." There had been a brief pause before she said, "Good night, Gregory. Sweet dreams." And then, the phone had died.

As painful as Kimberly walking out on him was, not hearing her return the words "I love you" had been a different kind of hurt. It was as if she had taken something vital from him, something irreplaceable. He wanted to drive over to the hotel, to demand she say the words, to stop this nonsense once and for all. He knew she loved him. Their love hadn't been the problem, but communication, neglect, and his own failings had poisoned their marriage. Though he wasn't the sole culprit, he knew he was the biggest offender.

Tears pricked at the back of his eyes, but he blinked them away. Crying was an admission of defeat, of not being able to fix things. He wasn't going to give in. He would fix this. He'd show Kimberly he could be the husband she deserved, that he could undo the damage he'd caused. He'd win back her trust, prove that his vows had never been broken.

"Please, God," he prayed silently, "let me convince her that I never betrayed her, that I never broke my vows with another woman."

That thought stayed with him as he made breakfast—his first time doing so in over thirty years. For all the little things Kimberly had done to make his life easier, he had never truly appreciated them. How had he been so blind to the way she cared for him? His conceit had led him to expect those things as though they were his due, not as a gift from her heart.

At work, he sat down to review his agenda. He couldn't afford to keep dwelling on his personal life, not today. He had a plan in place, and he needed to act. The woman trying to destroy his marriage was still out there, and it was time to set her up. Michael had already agreed to help, and together, they'd create the perfect trap. Gregory had no doubt that it would work. After all, someone was trying to undermine him, and he needed to know who.

The morning huddle in the break room was already underway when he arrived. The aroma of fresh coffee filled the air, mingling with the hum of voices. A few colleagues greeted him as he walked to the coffee machine. He glanced around the room. Josephine from the art department was there, someone who'd been with the company since its early days. She was as harmless as they came. Carol stood next to her; Gregory had little knowledge of her outside of the fact that she did her job well and had an extension close to his. Across the room, Angelica, his best friend's wife, chatted with some of the others. Though he knew she wasn't his culprit, it irked him to see her so calm and self-assured.

As he surveyed the room, he remembered something Michael had said: *Don't just focus on the women. Men can hide behind voices too.* With that in mind,

Gregory decided to bait the trap. He could already feel his heart race as he waited for his opening.

"So, before we dive into another day, does anyone have any exciting plans they want to share?" Gregory's voice cut through the buzz in the room. He watched his employees, assessing their reactions.

Most of them gave minimal answers, mentioning trivial things like Christmas plans or weekend activities. Gregory almost thought no one would bite, but then Angelica spoke up.

"What about you, oh illustrious leader? Any plans?"

It was the opening he needed.

"I'm going to a travel agent today to book a vacation." He chuckled lightly, as if it were a joke. "I'll surprise Kimberly later this year, so don't tell her!"

"What destination?" Angelica asked, her voice polite but seemingly uninterested.

"Ireland," he replied, his words slipping out before he could stop them. "Her mother was born there, and I want to take the entire family."

"Even her mother?" Angelica pressed, curiosity apparent in her tone. Kimberly's mother had always been a challenge for Gregory. He'd never fully earned her approval, no matter how hard he tried. Still, he did what he could to make her feel included in the family.

"It's for her mother, really. If I can't earn a few brownie points by taking her to Ireland, I might as well give up," he joked, but the words felt hollow.

He could sense the disinterest in the room as a few people murmured well wishes. But there was no one who seemed to care beyond the polite exchange. No one seemed to be taking the bait.

Gregory swallowed his frustration. His plan had barely made a ripple. But as he thought about it, he knew it would take more than a casual mention to bring the truth to light. His thoughts drifted back to Michael's suggestion of using a newer associate to gather intel.

Gregory pondered past employees who had left on bad terms, but none came to mind. He had worked hard to foster a company culture based on creativity and collaboration. He'd sent his staff on annual retreats, always focusing on their wellbeing and growth. Yet somehow, there was a leak—someone willing to destroy his marriage for reasons he couldn't yet understand.

As the huddle broke up and he returned to his office, Gregory felt the weight of the situation settle on his shoulders. The plan to uncover the culprit was set in motion, but he needed more time. He wanted to be sure, to understand the reasoning behind the betrayal.

He turned his attention to his team. Some were struggling financially. Gregory made a mental note to check in on them later. It was a small way to focus his energy on something productive. After all, if he couldn't solve his own problems, maybe he could help solve someone else's.

With a brief prayer for his team's wellbeing, Gregory instructed his assistant to send in the associate he had identified as having the greatest need. It wasn't a solution to the mess with Kimberly, but it was something.

Chapter Five

Kimberly

The phone conversation with Gregory last night brought back memories of better times, times she had long forgotten. Despite everything, despite how inattentive he had been, Gregory had never been a bad husband. She woke up with the sudden, startling realization that her love for him hadn't faded—it hadn't diminished at all. It still burned deep within her, a steady flame in the heart of all this confusion. He deserved a chance to defend himself.

She had treated him with little to no respect. Standing on her soapbox, spouting how she deserved more than what he had given her, it had all been so self-righteous. Why hadn't she just asked him after the first phone call? How had her unshakable belief in his innocence turned into such a firm conviction of his guilt? How did she end up leaving the house they had built together, a house she had spent decades perfecting?

Her life felt like it had spiraled out of control. The morning before Megan moved out, everything had made sense. Her husband had broken their vows, and she could no longer live with it. Yet, if she had done nothing, she would have slowly poisoned what little was left of their marriage with her insecurities. That suffocating desire for change gripped her again. She could not stay married to Gregory while his mistress flaunted their affair. But staying with him, loving a man she couldn't live with, seemed like a fate too grim to accept.

Why hadn't Father Rochelle blamed Gregory? Instead, he'd simply prayed with her, asking her to find the wisdom and peace she so desperately sought. Peace? That emotion had fled years ago, replaced by bitterness and suspicion.

All Kimberly wanted now was to know the truth. Each passing day left her less certain. She'd been away from Gregory for almost a week, and her once unshakable conviction in his guilt was starting to waver. The question—fight or flee—kept looping in her mind. Was their marriage worth saving, or had it truly reached its end? She had to decide. Make him stop cheating, or accept that he was. It would have been easier to deal with his infidelity if he'd admitted it. She would have preferred his confession over the endless denials.

Yet, as much as she wanted to believe in his guilt, a small part of her clung to the idea that maybe he didn't cheat. His denial, though far from comforting, did offer her a strange relief. Part of her fought against the lie he was telling her. Gregory had never been one to hide the truth, even when it hurt. She couldn't remember a time when he'd chosen deception over honesty.

One person knew the truth. But the thought of calling that woman—*the frustrating woman*—made Kimberly's teeth grind. She could use someone to talk to, someone who wasn't spiritually or emotionally invested in the well-being of her marriage. As she sat at the small dining table in her hotel suite, staring at the smartphone Gregory had bought for her when she'd dropped her old one in the lake, she wondered if speaking to Angelica was the answer. The phone had more bells and whistles than she cared to learn, but it could take photos and video calls with her children. It was a lifeline of sorts.

Before she could pick it up, the phone rang. Kimberly didn't need to check the screen to know it was Angelica. Sometimes there was nothing mysterious about the Lord's actions. The universe had decided today would be the day she'd talk to the wife of her husband's best friend. On the third ring, she pressed the button to accept the call and lifted the phone to her ear.

"Hello, Angelica," she greeted, her tone more pleasant than she felt.

"Have you lost your ever-loving mind?" Angelica's voice cracked through the phone, blunt and cutting. It wasn't the kindness Kimberly had come to expect from her. But rudeness? That was new.

"Excuse me?" The urge to press 'End Call' rose within her, but she stifled it. Angelica might have information that would put her mind to rest.

"I just got off the phone with the woman who claims to have information about Gregory's infidelity," Angelica went on, her tone laced with disgust. "Also, what kind of moron listens to a depraved digital voice for two years without at least punching her husband in the face?"

Kimberly froze. There was so much to unpack in Angelica's words. *How and why did Angelica accept a call meant for her?* And *why hadn't I confronted Gregory sooner?* The thought of punching him in the face had crossed her mind, but the reality of it was another story.

"I don't know what to say to that," Kimberly replied after the silence between them stretched long.

"I can help with that, too." Angelica's voice dripped with sarcasm. "You say, 'Angelica, I have no common sense and need your expertise in helping me plan a dinner date with my husband because I have a lot of words to say to him.'"

Kimberly regretted answering the phone. Angelica's voice, relentless in its truth, grated on her nerves. Part of why the two women had never been friends was how much Angelica reminded Kimberly of her mother. Her world wasn't big enough for two domineering women battling over who could tell Kimberly how she'd messed things up.

"What would you have done?" Kimberly asked, her tone sharper than she intended. But it was a question that needed an answer. Angelica was nothing if not direct.

"I wouldn't have waited two damn years," Angelica responded, without hesitation. "I mean, I know we aren't friends, but I'd have totally followed him around at night to uncover the truth. You could have at least asked if I saw anything suspicious at the office. I work one door down from your husband."

The thought of Kimberly and Angelica snooping around behind Gregory's back made her laugh, despite the tension in her chest. *This whole situation is insane.*

"If the roles were reversed, and someone called you about Michael, how would you have handled it?" Kimberly had to know. Though she couldn't match Angelica's boldness, hearing how another woman would have dealt with this mess might give her some clarity.

Angelica didn't hesitate. "Well, I'm not as nice as you. After the first phone call, I would have burned everything Michael owned on the front lawn while roasting marshmallows in nothing but his favorite tie and my best high heels. I'd want him to see what he threw away."

Kimberly inhaled too quickly and choked on her own breath. She couldn't even imagine doing something like that, not to Gregory.

"You'd really do that?" she asked, half-laughing, half-shocked.

"That's after I slashed all of his tires and broke every window on all three of his vehicles. Even if he's innocent, something in his world reached out to harm me. That puts the blame on him."

Angelica's unapologetic response made everything sound so simple. Kimberly was both disturbed and oddly impressed.

"Did you ever think you'd be calling me to tell me what a fool I've been?" Kimberly asked, though she wasn't sure she wanted an answer.

"I've wanted to make this call for years, but you've never done something as epically stupid as letting a viper into your marriage." Angelica's bored tone only fueled Kimberly's rising temper.

With her eyes closed, Kimberly pinched the bridge of her nose. "You make it so hard to like you."

"Wow, honesty, for the first time since I've known you. Tell me more," Angelica's voice shifted, a little too amused.

"You're a bully," Kimberly shot back, surprising herself with the honesty. "If someone has an idea that differs from yours, you browbeat them until they agree with you. Everything dissolves into a debate when you're involved."

"I'm a lawyer. That's my literal job description."

"Did you call me just to ask me if I'd lost my mind?" Kimberly's patience was wearing thin, and she fought the urge to hang up.

"I meant to invite you to lunch, honestly. You're just so prickly all the time, I can't help myself." Angelica's tone softened, like she was trying to make peace in her own way.

Kimberly's heart sank. She could feel how far she had fallen, and the pain of it hit her unexpectedly. She took a deep breath, and her voice softened. "Sushi?" she asked, trying to focus on something simple, something that could break the tension.

"Even better," Angelica replied. "Let's go get Pho soup at the local Vietnamese place. They don't mind if you sit at their table for an extended period. And you'll be spilling your guts before we plan the perfect date for you and Gregory. I'll text you the address. Be there in an hour."

Before Kimberly could respond, Angelica ended the call.

With a sigh, Kimberly stared at the phone in her hand, wondering if this was the beginning of something she couldn't control.

***

Gregory

With Michael's help, Gregory pored over every employee file from the last ten years. The task, tedious and methodical, carried an undercurrent of unease. Three years ago, he'd made the difficult decision to fire David Billings, after catching him embezzling company funds. It wasn't the first time David had tested the boundaries of trust. A few months before, David had stolen a small amount from the petty cash drawer. Enough to raise suspicion, but not so much as to guarantee detection. Gregory had given him another chance, knowing how life sometimes caught people off guard. But a month later, David had tried to take more—much more. The company's accountants noticed the sizeable theft almost immediately.

It was no longer about forgiveness. Gregory couldn't keep a man like that in his employ.

David was gone, but the trail didn't stop there. Carol Billings had come into the picture only six months after her husband's departure. Gregory had never made the connection between the two. Carol listed no spouse on her application, and though David's emergency contact was his wife, it had never seemed noteworthy. But now, after reviewing her file, everything was starting to add up. Carol had debts—a mountain of them—and the number she'd listed on her application matched the one in David's employment file. It was too much of a coincidence.

He had asked Emma to schedule a meeting with Carol for later that afternoon, hoping to discuss her situation and offer a company car until she could stabilize her finances. Michael had insisted that employees always have access to vehicles if needed, but Gregory was starting to wonder if his intentions were naive.

As a seasoned executive with decades in the business world, Gregory knew that his evidence was circumstantial. He needed more. He had to catch Carol in the act. But his instincts—shaped by years of experience—told him it was her. And still, a small part of him prayed he was wrong. Carol had worked for the company for three years without a single blemish on her record. She'd earned top marks in her evaluations and received the highest wage increases quarter after quarter.

But even the most reliable employees could have hidden lives, filled with desperate measures. He couldn't let it slide. He had no choice but to face the possibility that Carol was responsible for the destruction of his personal life.

Gregory paced his office, his mind racing. He had no idea if Michael's associate would get anything substantial from her, but he had to trust his instincts now. The pieces were falling into place, but nothing could prepare him for what was coming.

Michael finally entered unannounced, Carol in tow. She stormed into the room, visibly disheveled, her usual polished exterior crumbling under the weight of her situation. The anger in her voice took him off guard, but he couldn't let his surprise show.

"Let me go, jerk," she hissed, slumping into one of the chairs his wife, Kimberly, had chosen for the office. Gregory noted the unkempt state of her clothes, the way her blazer was askew, as though the very fabric of her life was unraveling.

"I have rights. If you touch me again, I'll sue you for assault and wrongful imprisonment," she spat, her gaze unwavering and cold.

"We observed you using the office phone on the second floor to call my house phone. Angelica took the call and heard you discussing a trip Gregory is planning with his mistress," Michael explained calmly, though his voice had an edge to it.

Gregory had expected anger. He'd anticipated confrontation. But what he felt was something far worse—deep disappointment. This was a woman who had worked for him, who had made promises to herself and the company she betrayed. He'd thought he knew her.

"Do you know why you're here?" Gregory asked, his voice steady despite the churn of emotions rising within him. Anger. Hurt. A fear he hadn't been able to shake since this whole mess began.

"Do I look stupid to you?" Carol sneered. "As golden boy said, I'm the one who called your wife." She made a show of glaring at him, her voice dripping with sarcasm. "Did she leave you? I wondered when it would happen. So much for your perfect little world."

Gregory's heart thudded in his chest. His marriage, the one thing he'd always tried to protect, was now caught in the web of betrayal. But he couldn't afford to get lost in her venomous words. Not now. Not when there was still hope.

"Carol, what possessed you to do such a thing?" His voice caught, as if the question had weight he hadn't anticipated.

Her anger was raw. "You ruined my life! My husband turned to the bottle after you fired him. Do you know what it's like to live with someone who doesn't care about you? Who drinks himself stupid every day? You did that to him!" Spittle flew from her lips as her eyes burned with a fury Gregory wasn't sure how to combat.

There was a part of him that wanted to retaliate, to rip into her with the anger she deserved. But instead, a strange, unfamiliar sympathy surged within him. In that moment, Gregory could see how desperate she was, how broken. And that anger she aimed at him wasn't just about him. It was about years of pain that had nothing to do with his decisions.

"I'll give you six weeks severance pay," he said, his tone controlled, but the bitterness still lingered. "It's more than you deserve for what you did to my wife. The pain and torture you've caused her is something I'll never easily forgive. But I will pray for you, Carol. I hope you find peace."

He meant it. Despite everything, he meant it.

She stood up abruptly, her shoulders tense, and stormed out of his office. Michael followed behind, his presence like a shadow at Gregory's back.

"Pick up your check at the receptionist's office," Gregory called after her. "And clear your personal effects out in the next five minutes. If you ever return, I'll have you arrested for trespassing."

A silence settled over the room after they left, and it wasn't the kind of silence that offered comfort. Gregory's chest ached, weighed down by the consequences of his actions. Even with the proof he now had, with everything lining up in his favor to clear his name, it didn't feel like a victory.

"Head's up. Kimberly will arrive in a few hours," Michael's voice broke through the quiet.

Gregory's heart skipped a beat, and he felt an unfamiliar sense of hope. Kimberly was coming. He didn't know what to expect, but it was a chance—a slim one, but a chance nonetheless.

"How's this tie?" Gregory asked, pulling at the fabric around his neck as if it could offer him some kind of reassurance.

"Stop worrying," Michael said, stepping back with a knowing smile. "Angelica is running interference until we get everything in place. But she said you owe her a week at your cabin."

A week. A lifetime ago, the four of them—Gregory, Kimberly, Michael, and Angelica—had spent weekends in the mountains, trying to escape the chaos of their lives. That was before everything became tangled up in lies, before the work he should have kept separate from his marriage had consumed him.

Gregory caught a glimpse of himself in the mirror above the sink, fixing his tie with a quiet resolve.

"God," he whispered to his reflection, "give me the wisdom to speak the truth to her. To open her heart to what I need her to understand."

His faith had seen him through the hardest times. He could only pray it would carry him through the storm ahead.

Chapter Six

Kimberly

Lunch with Angelica left Kimberly emotionally drained. Hearing her fears spoken aloud by someone else—someone who knew her so well—was a painful revelation. The Vietnamese soup she'd enjoyed earlier felt like lead in her stomach, heavy as she processed all that Angelica had forced her to face. The truth about her own faults in the marriage was a bitter pill to swallow.

"Not a drop of dye in sight," Angelica commented, admiring Kimberly's natural hair. "I'd give anything to have this color." Kimberly barely noticed the tresses anymore. When Gregory's attention wasn't on her, she'd lost the desire to care about her appearance.

After lunch, Angelica insisted on a stop at a boutique that specialized in head-to-toe transformations.

"Thank you," Kimberly said, though the word felt heavy on her tongue.

"Holiday party?" Angelica asked, glancing over as Kimberly received her makeover.

In the next chair, Angelica, too, was getting pampered. After spending the better part of thirty minutes pointing out Kimberly's cowardice, Angelica softened, confessing her desire to be a better friend.

"No," Kimberly replied, her tone shifting, "more like a date."

Angelica raised an eyebrow. "Oh? A hot night on the town?"

"With my husband." Kimberly glanced at herself in the mirror, surprised by the woman staring back at her. She hadn't seen this version of herself in a long time.

Yes, she would fix her marriage. The first step was acknowledging that she had given up her voice, embracing the role of the victim. Angelica had been brutally honest, tearing down the weak parts of Kimberly's character. Though the truth stung, it was the kind of wake-up call she needed.

With a fresh haircut and her nails gleaming with a manicure, Angelica led her to the evening dress section to find something that would dazzle Gregory. If anyone had told Kimberly she'd be taking fashion advice from Angelica, she would have laughed.

Angelica had dropped a bombshell when she bluntly pointed out one simple fact: Kimberly had never fought for her marriage. Instead, she had embraced a narrative that let someone else turn her into a victim. There were moments during lunch when Kimberly hated the woman holding up the mirror, but those moments were fewer than the ones spent hating the woman in the reflection.

Today, that image would be shattered. No more silent suffering, no more talking about separations or divorce. Tonight would be about rebirth—about rekindling the love they once had and placing it at the center of their lives.

"You look stunning," said the boutique stylist as Kimberly stepped out of the dressing room, Angelica smirking beside her.

"Thank you," Kimberly said, a blush creeping up her cheeks as she took in the sight of herself in the mirror.

"I mean it," the stylist continued. "It's as if the designer made this dress just for you." Her eyes gleamed with approval. "I know exactly what you need for this look. I'll be right back."

"There she is," Angelica said, eyes alight with admiration. "The woman I met so long ago. The only woman in the world who intimidated me."

Kimberly's gaze lingered in the mirror. The dress was a soft sea-green that crisscrossed over her front, revealing a hint of cleavage. The straps tied delicately behind her neck, and the back was bare, falling straight to her ankles. In its simplicity, it was beautiful.

"I intimidated you?" Kimberly turned to face her friend, her voice laced with surprise.

"Uh, yeah," Angelica replied, a teasing glint in her eyes. "You're a nightmare in heels when you decide someone isn't worth your time."

Tears pricked Kimberly's eyes, her character stripped bare yet again. "And yet, you're still here, teaching me how to be a better woman, wife, and apparently, a better human. Is there anything else you'd like to get off your chest?"

Angelica smiled, but the words that followed were unflinching. "Just stop being a selfish jerk and maybe let the world in once in a while." Her tone was light, but the sincerity rang through.

Before Kimberly could respond, the stylist returned with boxes of shoes and jewelry. "I wasn't sure what size you wore, so I grabbed a few options."

Kimberly slipped on a pair of clear heels with a green heel that matched the dress perfectly. They reminded her of Cinderella's glass slipper.

"These are perfect," she said, her voice thick with emotion. "Thank you."

"I thought silver would complement the dress best," the stylist said, offering a set of teardrop emerald earrings in a soft silver setting. She completed the look with a matching necklace. Kimberly hesitated, glancing at the price tag.

"Try them on with the dress first," the stylist suggested. "I have a feeling they'll be worth every penny."

Kimberly donned the earrings and necklace, her heart skipping a beat as she checked her reflection. The transformation was undeniable. The dress, the jewelry, the shoes—she felt like someone else entirely. The woman in the mirror was confident, radiant, a stranger she almost didn't recognize.

She stood taller, proud of the woman she saw before her. Gregory wasn't the only one to blame for the rift in their marriage. It took two to cause the distance between them, and she was ready to fight for them both.

"I know you may think I'm just trying to make a sale," the stylist said, her voice warm. "But if you'd like, we can finish your look with makeup. It's rare we get to send a fairy princess off to meet her handsome prince."

"I'd like that," Kimberly said, a playful smile tugging at her lips. "Let's just hope he doesn't turn into a frog when he sees the bill."

The stylist smiled again. "The last thing he'll be thinking about when he sees you is a bill. Besides, it's not every day we get to see a marriage as it was meant to be."

Kimberly closed her eyes, fighting the urge to stomp her foot in frustration. Another reminder of what she'd neglected. If her daughters learned that their mother had silently assumed the worst about her husband for two years, they might start to use silence as a shield.

She felt the stylist's brush sweep over her face, dabbing and blending with skill. Kimberly leaned back, savoring the brief silence as she collected herself.

"Oh, I'm sorry!" the stylist said, her voice apologetic as a powder puff brushed Kimberly's face, causing her to sneeze.

"Don't worry," Kimberly said quickly, not wanting to make the woman feel worse. "It's nothing. I have a daughter, a little older than you. Her go-to response to everything is an apology. Powder in the nose will always trigger that reaction. But you should know, it's important to hoard the power we're given as women. Apologies are a sign of guilt, and that takes away from our power. Take it from me, someone who almost threw away thirty years of marriage because I didn't fight for myself. Hoard your power. It's a precious commodity."

The stylist paused, considering the words. "Then I take back my apology and I'll just say, you good?"

Kimberly smiled. "I'm excellent."

***

Gregory

"Are you sure about this? I mean, this will bombard her publicly," Michael asked for the third time that evening.

"No, I'm not. But it's what I need to do." Gregory tried to ignore the lingering doubt that kept him second guessing his actions. He watched as men wielding hammers built a pagoda with white lace and white tea lights glinting in the darkening sky.

What he was about to do went beyond besieging his wife. It left him wide open to ridicule and gossip for ages. He based all his hope on the love he had for his wife.

With the help of his friends, he'd organized a moment he hoped would put an end to any talk of separation. After they escorted Carol off the premises, he began making phone calls. He called all their friends, family, children, and church members. He begged, pleaded, and outright bribed everyone into helping him create a miracle in one day.

Throughout the day, he prayed for guidance and wisdom. Michael stood by his side, even when he didn't agree with what Gregory was doing. To his surprise, Angelica handled most of the details that had never occurred to him with her cell phone while at the salon with Kimberly.

As if aware of his thoughts, Michael said, "If you're reading this wrong, you'll be praying to keep her from killing you. What would you have done if she came straight here?"

"I trusted your wife. If there's one thing that gives Kimberly courage in the face of danger, hope when all seems lost, and happiness on a cloudy day, it's shopping. It never takes her less than five hours to shop." Gregory chuckled. He neglected to mention that he also checked online to view the locations of credit card uses. It never failed to amaze him how quickly credit card statements showed up on the Internet.

"There goes your retirement fund." Michael laughed.

Gregory shrugged his shoulders and shook his head. "Some investments are well worth it." Another lesson he'd learned from Kimberly's departure. No amount of savings would fill the drive he had within him because money had no spiritual value. Never again would he define his worth by the amount of money in his bank account.

"I'm happy for you. Embrace your second chance, my friend. You deserve it." Michael threw him the small box that held Kimberly's new wedding ring. It wasn't fancy, just a simple platinum band to show his eternal love for her.

"I just wish it had never come to this."

"I understand. But sometimes the big man upstairs does something drastic to get our attention. Don't blow it this time."

"Never again, my friend. Never again." Gregory meant every word.

The rest of the afternoon turned into a whirlwind of activity. He enlisted the help of his daughters. They were ecstatic at the idea. A surprise party for their mother set them into a flurry of action.

Gregory was grateful for the people he had in his life. Everyone from their church was decorating, cooking, and whipping his backyard into a sea of white and green. Kimberly loved green, and he hoped the white would represent renewal. He wanted to signify a rebirth of his marriage. Faith and love were two things he and Kimberly had in abundance, kept him going despite what had threatened to tear their life apart.

He swore everyone to secrecy. They thought it was because he wanted to surprise her. In all honesty, it was because he was afraid if she had prior knowledge she'd run for the hills.

Each time fear crept into his heart, he pushed it out, hoping Kimberly would realize what they had. He refused to believe she could walk away from all of it without a backwards glance.

"You want me to hang in the back to make sure Carol doesn't cause a scene?" Michael asked.

"No. Your place is beside me. Nothing has changed."

"What if she shows up?" Unwilling to let go of his concern, Michael persisted. "She did not leave willingly. I had to involve the authorities."

"I'm sorry to hear the situation involved the police, but if she finds her way here, Megan will block her entry," Gregory chuckled. "Then Grace will probably do something reckless, like slash her tires."

Though he said it jokingly, Gregory was certain that if someone tried to ruin this day, his daughter would make them rue their birth.

His mother-in-law walked into the den. Even pushing eighty, she still scared the daylights out of him. Mona Kilbane eyed him with the same suspicion she'd had the day he'd met her. He still didn't know where he stood with her, but only Kimberly's opinion mattered to him.

"What's the big rush? I've seen shot-gun weddings that had more time to prepare," she asked him. "What did you do?" Mona got straight to the point, as was her nature. It galled him he would have to answer her because she probably knew anyway. Kimberly kept little from her mother.

Gregory wasn't sure how to answer her. Part of him wanted to lie and say it was just a grandiose gesture of love to his wife. The other part knew this tiny Irish woman would call him out on it.

"Kimberly left me last week. Manipulated by one of my employees into believing I cheated on her. I'm doing the only thing I can think of to show her how much I love her." The words came out in a rush, as if breathing would stop their flow.

"Good for you." With that, she patted his hand. She opened her arms to him and beckoned him to enter her embrace. After she hugged him, she walked away. Gregory stared after her, stunned. In thirty years, she'd tolerated him, but never had she offered him her affection.

"Dad, your tux is here. I put it up in your room. Angelica called and you have about twenty minutes before they leave the salon," Megan said from the doorway. He smiled at her as his nerves unraveled.

"What if she hates all this? What if she turns and walks away?" He asked as fear rose his spine. Even though he held firm in his faith, it terrified him she could just turn away and leave him for good.

Both Michael and Megan stared at him. "I'll tackle her to the ground and Grace will tie her up. The priest will guilt her and Devon will brow beat her. Don't worry, daddy, we've got this covered." Megan winked at him. "Now go get changed."

Gregory couldn't help but laugh at the image his daughter presented. As he walked up the stairs to his bedroom, he talked to his maker the entire way. He needed the strength to prove to his wife his unwavering devotion to her and their marriage.

As panicked thoughts set in, he allowed them to roll off him. Was he doing the right thing? Was this too much, too soon? He had less than half an hour to convince his wife he had never cheated on her, propose to her, convince her to stay with him for the rest of their lives, and then renew their vows in front of all their guests.

"Why couldn't I just ask her on another date?" he asked aloud. Michael had asked him the same thing. The answer was so simple.

He refused to spend any more time away from his wife. He didn't want to sleep alone in a bed meant for the two of them. Never again would he settle to wake up without her warm body next to his. He wanted to resolve the issue in their lives, and he wanted to do it all at once. Patience had never been one of his virtues. If she ended their marriage, he'd start a fresh one with her as a man bent on redemption.

If she didn't think he loved her, she would know after he declared it before all their friends and family. If she didn't think she could trust him, he'd build her trust all over again. One day at a time for the rest of their lives. If she didn't think she could share a life with him, he'd show her that a life without him in it wasn't worth striving for.

There was nothing he wouldn't do to remind the woman he loved what she meant to him. If she didn't have faith in their relationship that allowed her to bring her fears or concerns to him, he'd vow it before everyone they knew that he'd carry all her burdens. Even those he caused.

Public shame wouldn't deter him. Most of the men in the group fell into the same boat as him. They worked too hard and took their wives for granted. If his gesture could help someone else, then he'd allow the scare of humiliation to serve as a reminder to others. He embraced the opportunity to help others from falling into the same patterns as him.

Chapter Seven

Kimberly

After Angelica helped Kimberly settle into the car, being careful not to wrinkle her dress, the two women set off toward Kimberly's house. Angelica had convinced her that the best course of action was to show up and demand Gregory take her out on a date. She'd even thought to bring a corsage, ready to pin it to whatever attire he was wearing.

As they turned onto Kimberly's street, the sight of cars lined up around the block caught her off guard. "Of all days for someone to have a party," Kimberly muttered under her breath. The sheer volume of vehicles—sedans, trucks, and SUVs—lined the street, spilling over and blocking a few driveways. Her neighbors would be furious.

"Drive up on the lawn," Kimberly instructed when they couldn't find a spot to park. Her SUV, built for situations like this, would manage just fine.

Angelica drove over the curb, parking the vehicle on the grass. She checked the visor mirror, making sure her makeup and hair were still intact. Nerves crept in, but she wasn't surprised. She wanted to look perfect for Gregory. They deserved the life they'd once dreamed of—one that had slipped away because he'd buried himself in work and she hadn't fought for herself, or for their marriage.

Kimberly got out of the car, careful not to let her new heels sink into the soft grass. Angelica moved ahead, pressing the doorbell in rapid succession. Kimberly opened her mouth to tell her the house key was in her hand, but before she could speak, the front door opened to reveal her youngest daughter, Megan, wearing a formal dress.

Kimberly's stomach dropped. She bit her lip to suppress a groan. She had hoped to have a quiet moment with Gregory, to talk about everything that had happened, and what she dreamed would come next. But seeing Megan—whom she hadn't seen in a week—shifted her focus.

"Hi, Mama!" Megan exclaimed, her face lighting up. "Wow! You look stunning! I heard you were out shopping for presents. I thought they were for us, not your body!" Her infectious smile made Kimberly forget, for a moment, the whirlwind she had walked into.

"Shopping for presents?" Kimberly frowned, confused as she pulled Megan into an embrace.

"Isn't that where you've been this week? Off to Pittsburgh for last-minute holiday shopping?" Megan asked, pulling back and giving her mother a puzzled look.

Kimberly mumbled something that sounded vaguely like agreement. It wasn't surprising Gregory had come up with a plausible excuse to explain her absence without embarrassing her in front of the children.

"Oh! Come see something," Megan said, grabbing Kimberly's hand and leading her toward the backyard. "You'll love it!"

"Where's your father?" Kimberly asked casually, trying to mask her growing curiosity.

"He's around. Come on!" Megan tugged her forward, and Kimberly followed.

As they reached the back door, her breath caught in her throat. The backyard had been transformed into something almost unreal. Rows of chairs, draped with white taffeta and adorned with green bows, lined the path. Green and white flower petals were scattered down the aisle, which led to a small altar.

Kimberly's mind spun. "What on earth…?"

"Surprise!" The voices of friends and family rang out joyfully from the yard, and Kimberly stood frozen, her gaze scanning faces she hadn't seen in years.

"I... I don't understand," she whispered, trying to take everything in. This was more than she had bargained for.

Before she could process further, a familiar voice called out from behind her.

"Kimberly."

Her heart skipped. She turned to find Gregory standing there, dressed formally, his face full of love and anticipation.

"Gregory, what's going on?" she asked, needing him to anchor her in the surreal moment.

"Every day, I wake up thinking of you. Every night, before I sleep, I pray for you. And every night, while I'm asleep, I dream of you," he said softly, his voice carrying the weight of years spent apart.

Her breath caught in her throat as his words stirred emotions she had long buried. "When I'm away from you, I want nothing more than to be beside you. When I'm afraid, I want your strength. When I'm happy, I want your laughter. It has taken me three decades to realize how much you mean to me." He paused, eyes searching hers.

The world around them faded as he continued, "I know this is unexpected. I know we have issues to address, but I don't want to face them alone."

Gregory then lowered himself to one knee, and Kimberly's breath hitched.

"Kimberly, my beautiful Kimberly. Will you do me the honor of renewing our vows? Marry me again, and let's face the rest of our days, loving each other."

The crowd fell silent. Kimberly's thoughts whirled, caught between disbelief and the dawning realization that this was real. Gregory was asking her to marry him again.

"Nothing in this world would give me greater pleasure," she said, her voice barely above a whisper, as she opened her fingers to let him slide the ring above the one she had never taken off.

A cheer erupted from the crowd as Gregory leaned in to kiss her forehead. "The next one will be in front of the priest," he teased, winking at her. For a moment, their past troubles seemed distant, dissolving in the warmth of his love.

Just then, a voice shouted from behind them.

"I'm here! I'm here!"

Kimberly turned to see her son Devon running toward them, struggling to tie a bowtie around his neck. "I couldn't help with the planning, but I promised Dad I'd be here in time to give the bride away. I'm not too late, am I?"

Kimberly couldn't help but laugh at the sight of him. Tears welled up in her eyes as she wiped them away, hoping her makeup would survive the moment.

"You're right on time," Gregory said with a grin, turning toward their son.

Gregory took Kimberly's hand and pressed something into her palm. She opened her hand to reveal a small charm shaped like a doghouse.

"What's this?" she asked, confused.

"It's a reminder," Gregory said, his tone lighthearted. "When I do something stupid—and we both know I will—you can put me in there."

He pointed to a small fenced-in shed at the edge of the yard, the words "Gregory's Doghouse" painted in bold letters above the door.

"I love you, Kimberly," he said. "Thank you for loving me enough to stand here with me."

"My place is beside you," she replied softly, though she still didn't quite understand the charm's meaning.

"Well, technically, right now, your place is with Devon," Gregory said, nudging her toward their son.

Her heart full, Kimberly linked her arm with Devon's as he led her down the aisle. The soft crunch of rose petals beneath her Cinderella shoes was drowned out by the sound of the wedding march playing in the background. Camera flashes popped around her, but she only had eyes for her son.

Kimberly was in awe. Gregory had planned an entire wedding in one day. The thought of how much he believed in their love, how far he was willing to go to rekindle it, overwhelmed her.

As she reached the front, Father Rochelle smiled at her and addressed the gathered crowd. "Friends and family of Gregory and Kimberly, today we witness the renewal of their faith and love in the bonds of their marriage."

Kimberly turned toward Gregory, taking both of his hands in hers as Father Rochelle began the vows.

"Do you take Gregory Davenport as your lawful husband, to have and to hold, for better or for worse, for richer or for poorer, in sickness and in health, to love and cherish until death do you part?"

Memories of their original wedding day flooded her heart. This was right. She could feel it in her bones.

"I do," Kimberly answered, her voice steady. "I take this ring as a sign of my love and faithfulness, in the name of the Father, the Son, and the Holy Spirit."

"Do you take Kimberly Davenport as your lawful wife, to have and to hold, for better or for worse, for richer or for poorer, in sickness and in health, to love and cherish until death do you part?"

"I do," Gregory's voice rang out, strong and certain.

When Father Rochelle announced, "You may kiss the bride," Kimberly's heart fluttered, and she felt like she might swoon. This moment was everything.

***

Gregory

The day had been perfect, surrounded by friends and family, basking in the kind of joy only a wedding could bring. It was a day neither of them would ever forget. Yet, as the last of their guests left, an unexpected silence settled over the house, and Kimberly stood there, her mind racing. She knew there was something important to say, but she wasn't sure where to begin.

Gregory had gone to take a shower, leaving her in his office. She paced restlessly, her thoughts tangled, trying to form the words that felt so important but elusive. Her eyes landed on the wastebasket in the corner, and for reasons she couldn't explain, it held her attention.

She took a few steps forward and noticed a crumpled piece of paper peeking out from the top. That wasn't like Gregory. He was meticulous about keeping everything organized, especially documents. The pile in the trash was unusual—too much paper for someone as thorough as him.

Curiosity led her to retrieve the documents, smoothing them out carefully. As she read, her pulse quickened. The pages were filled with telephone records—each one marked with a single number highlighted in bright ink. Her stomach dropped as she realized the number came from an extension in Gregory's office.

Before she could even make sense of it, a voice interrupted her thoughts.

"Your mystery woman called after you left. I heard the torture she put you through. I'm so sorry you had to go through that, and even worse, that you went through it alone. It was Michael's idea to pull the phone records to see who it was."

Gregory stood in the doorway, fresh from the shower, his towel hanging low on his hips. Water droplets clung to his skin, and for a moment, Kimberly couldn't focus on anything but the sight of him. She lowered the documents, embarrassment creeping over her like a cold wave. She didn't need more proof of her own foolishness. The shredder hummed to life as she slid the papers inside, the mechanical sound filling the silence between them.

"Why did you throw it away?" Gregory asked softly, his gaze steady but laced with something she couldn't quite place.

She swallowed, struggling to hold herself together. "I wanted a life with you based on love. I didn't need a piece of paper to tell me I didn't cheat on you."

The weight of her own stupidity pressed heavily on her chest. She could have uncovered the truth herself, if only she'd trusted him, if only she'd thought it through. How lucky she was that he could forgive so easily.

Her face flushed with shame, but the truth of what had happened, of everything Angelica had said about her, hit her like a punch to the gut. She had almost lost everything. Everything that mattered.

"Oh God, Gregory," she whispered, her voice breaking as she looked at him. "What have I done?"

She felt the urge to run, to escape the reality of what she'd almost destroyed. But the questions, the whys that swirled in her mind, wouldn't leave her. Why had Angelica done it? Why had she worked so hard to try to tear their marriage apart?

Gregory moved toward her, his hands gentle as he cupped her face, forcing her to meet his eyes.

"We both have things we wish we'd done differently, Kimberly. But that was yesterday. Today is our wedding day. And only the future lies ahead of us. The past can't harm us now."

"But why?" she asked again, her voice full of hurt. "Why would she spend all that time trying to destroy us?"

Gregory sighed, his eyes distant for a moment, before he turned back to her. "It's a sad story. One I'd rather not repeat. Our love was a bone of contention for her. She was jealous."

He paused, his expression shifting as if he were reconsidering his words. "No. Let me be completely honest. I had to let her husband go from his position. He spiraled after that. Alcohol took over, and he lost everything—his family, his life. It's a sad, messy situation, but there are no heroes or villains here, just circumstances beyond anyone's control."

Kimberly didn't know what to say. That was a long time to focus on someone else, a long time to hold on to bitterness.

"And a long time to believe lies," Gregory added softly. She nestled closer to him, her head resting against his chest, and the warmth of his embrace wrapped around her like a shield.

"So, what now?" she asked, her voice small.

"Now we live. Really live. We embrace love and faith because we have an abundance of both. Today is our second chance, Kimberly. And we're going to make the most of it."

She could feel his hands gently holding hers, his touch comforting, a reassurance that they were in this together. Her heart pounded as she lifted her face to his, yearning for the kiss she knew was coming.

His lips met hers gently at first, then deepened as he pulled her closer, his hands in her hair. The kiss was everything she'd wanted—tender, yet fierce, full of all the things they hadn't said.

They pulled away, breathless. Gregory's smile was all she needed to see. It was a smile that told her everything: he had never stopped loving her, and he never would.

"What's so funny?" Gregory asked, his eyes wide in mock confusion as she began to laugh.

"A wedding, Gregory?" Kimberly wiped away the tears that had sprung to her eyes, her laugh uncontrollable now. "What if I had said no?"

He raised an eyebrow, then smirked. "I'm a lawyer, Kimberly. I'm good at convincing people to agree to my demands. Besides, I wanted a honeymoon."

She gasped. "We're going on a honeymoon?"

"Yes. I've been planning it for a while. Ireland. Your mother always talked about wanting to go back. I thought it would be the perfect vacation. I know I should've planned it years ago, but work always seemed to get in the way. That will never happen again."

Kimberly blinked, surprised. "We're going to Ireland?"

"Yes. And we're taking your father, your mother, Megan, Grace, and Devon too," he said with a chuckle. "Maybe honeymoon isn't the right word, but it will be the best family vacation we've ever had. Maybe Michael and Angelica will join us too—after all, they helped make today happen."

Kimberly laughed again. "Honeymoon Davenport style, complete with friends and family in tow."

Gregory gave her a serious look then, his expression turning slightly more somber. "I have one question."

Her heart skipped a beat as she gazed up at him. "What?"

"Do you trust me?"

The question, full of raw vulnerability, hit her like a thunderclap. For a moment, she couldn't breathe.

"I trust you, Gregory," she said softly, her voice cracking as the weight of everything finally hit her. "Can you ever forgive me for not believing in you?"

He shook his head, pulling her into his arms once more. "There's nothing to forgive. Our adventure starts now. This is our new beginning. Today, God gave us a miracle. A new chapter, Kimberly."

She looked up at him, her heart full, and whispered, "I love you, Gregory."

He smiled down at her, love radiating from his eyes. "I love you, today, tomorrow, and forever. This is just the beginning, Kimberly. Our next thirty years start now."

Hand in hand, they walked to their bedroom. She turned off the lights, and as they climbed into bed together, the future seemed bright, filled with the promise of love, trust, and the adventure they were about to embark on.

About the Author

Kristy Kelly wears many hats. She's the mother of four children who are adults. The ever-loving grandmother of children she strives to spoil at every available opportunity. Her journey into writing started when she was around fourteen and filled spiral notebooks with endless stories that she'd one day send off to Harlequin Romance. Her parents, supportive of her writing, bought her an electronic typewriter. While she never made it to Harlequin, she uncovered a passion for sharing her stories with others.

She lives in Kinston, North Carolina and spends her days writing. A frequent contributor to Neuse News, Kristy enjoys writing about events that impact rural North Carolina. When she's not writing tales or news, she's often found fishing on the Neuse River, kayaking, or camping. She tried hiking, but it wasn't her thing at all, and she decided they made vehicles for a reason.

As a person with Obsessive Compulsive Disorder, and Attention Deficit Disorder, finishing projects are often a challenge for Kristy, but she strives to write each day to continue to develop her skill and find new fans. If you liked what you read, or want to know more, you can find her at https://kris tykelly.com or on social media; Facebook @authorkristydkelly, Instagram @authorkristydkelly. She loves to hear from anyone who reads her book and looks forward to writing fresh stories for people to fall in love with.

Perhaps one day she'll write for Harlequin, but for today, she writes for her readers, hoping she brings joy to anyone who reads the words that escaped from her mind and onto a screen. Her favorite authors are Neil Gaiman, Douglas Adams, and Molly Harper. If you see her online, please let her know what you thought of the book.

Read more from Kristy Kelly

Blown Away

Chapter One

Oh, how far the mighty have fallen.

The words reverberated through Derek "Dash" Jarvis's mind as he finished his last song of the night at the only dive bar in town that would still let him play. Once the darling of Nashville, the man who had graced the stages of sold-out arenas, he now played for the rough-and-rowdy crowds who didn't care about his ruined reputation. The indignation churned in his gut like acid, but he plastered on a smile and thanked the few dozen people who still bothered to show up.

The crowd cheered wildly, their energy a bittersweet reminder of what once was. It might not have been the Grand Ole Opry, but their applause, the thunder of it, made him feel like a star again.

"Dash! Dash! Dash!"

Their chants were like a balm to his wounded spirit. Even when his words had fallen on deaf ears, the music always spoke louder. The paparazzi could drag his name through the mud with half-truths and outright lies, but with a single strum of his guitar, he could change opinions, one person at a time.

"You all have been amazing!" he shouted into the mic, his voice thick with emotion.

When he had first been asked to play at this small bar, Derek had wanted to refuse. It reminded him too much of where he'd started—before the fame, before everything fell apart. Coming back felt like another slap in the face. But in the end, he couldn't turn down the chance to play.

He turned to his lead guitarist. "You killed it tonight."

"Talk to them, man. Show 'em that Southern charm!" his guitarist replied with a grin.

Derek took a deep breath, his gaze sweeping over the crowd. He smiled at the ragtag group of people under the hazy yellow lights. "Thank you for having me here tonight!" he said, his voice rough but sincere.

Then, from the back of the room, a voice called out: "We don't care what Alexa Vasquez says—we love you, Dash!"

Derek froze. Alexa Vasquez. The Gossip Queen. She had made it her life's mission to tear him down, to take his every misstep and turn it into a spectacle. No matter what he did, no matter how much he tried to redeem himself, she always found a way to make him look worse. He'd never understood how one person could wage such a relentless war against him—and win.

The anger burned deep, but he forced out a laugh. "Don't worry. Tomorrow, you'll read about how I couldn't even remember the words to my own songs because I was so drunk or high." The crowd laughed, but Derek knew that it was likely she would twist his words into exactly that. "I love this place, I love this crowd, and I love playing for you."

The only high he'd ever chased was the rush after a great night on stage. The endorphins from the music, the connection with the crowd—nothing else compared.

As the crew packed up the gear, Derek made his way around, shaking hands and thanking them. He owed everything to his band and crew, and he never wanted them to forget that. They'd been with him through thick and thin for the last decade, and without them, he was nothing.

When he stepped down from the stage, a few fans gathered around him.

Gone were the days when he'd be rushed off to a private room. Now, he stopped to sign autographs and chat. The fact that people still wanted his signature, still wanted to talk to him, meant more than he cared to admit.

A pretty blonde handed him a piece of paper. "Thank you so much for tonight. I'm going to blog about how amazing you were."

"Well, darling, I'd appreciate that. Thanks for coming out," Derek said with a smile. He turned to walk away, but she grabbed his arm.

"I know you don't know me, but you'll remember my face. Just remember Tennessee Titan," she said with a wink before letting go of his arm.

He had no idea what she meant, but the intensity in her eyes made him believe her. "Just by being here, enjoying the music… that's all I need to remember you."

Derek worked the crowd as he always did—one person at a time. He might never reclaim the vast audience he once had, but every person he won over was a victory. Playing for people, for real fans, was all he had ever wanted.

By the time he climbed into his tour bus, Derek felt like he'd made a small dent in the world that had written him off. He longed for sleep, to forget about the grind for just a few hours. But as soon as his head hit the pillow, his phone rang.

It was 4:30 in the morning.

"Hello?" he answered, groggy and irritated.

"Hey, Dash," a familiar voice said, and he couldn't help but smile. Kimberly Ridder, his steadfast record label rep, was one of the few people who still believed in him.

"Hi, Kimmy. I'm guessing you're not calling with good news."

"Did you actually say you were too high to remember the words to your own songs?" she asked, a note of humor in her voice, but also a hint of reproach. She'd warned him time and again not to give the tabloids ammunition.

"Damn," he muttered. "I didn't… I wasn't high."

"Look, I just got off the phone with Edward Dalton," she said, her voice flat. "He wants to cut you loose."

Her words hit him like a freight train. Without a record label, he was finished. No one would want him without the backing of Bluegrass Records.

"Kimmy, I wasn't high," he said, his throat tight with emotion.

"It doesn't matter, Dash," she replied, her voice heavy with finality. "You're a liability now."

His heart sank. "When?"

"Be at the office tomorrow at noon," she said, and the line went dead.

He hurled the phone across the room, the sound of it crashing against the walls almost as loud as the agony in his chest.

Meanwhile, across town, Jessica Hartford wasn't having a much better morning. As she dug through her second-hand Coach bag, her fingers closed around the small morsels of semi-sweet chocolate that were her only solace. She popped one into her mouth and let it melt, savoring the brief moment of peace.

Her client sat across from her, his handsome face betraying nothing of the storm inside. Jessica had agreed to represent him, to help salvage his career after his ex-wife's vicious smear campaign. The internet had been brutal—nothing but lies about pornography and deviant behavior.

"Let's see if we've achieved our goals," Jessica said, flipping open her laptop with a calmness she didn't feel.

Her client sighed. "Miss Hartford, no matter what the outcome, I just want you to know how much I appreciate everything you've done. You've gone above and beyond."

Jessica's heart clenched, but she kept her focus. "I'm sure the high road we've taken with your ex-wife will pay off." She hit the button to start the projector.

The first website came up, and her client's name gleamed across the top of the page. Beneath it was a glowing article, praising his artistic talent and his humanitarian efforts. Even better—one of the most notorious gossip bloggers had recanted her earlier story.

Jessica exhaled in relief as more positive articles followed. Her client leapt out of his seat, grinning ear to ear. He scooped her up in a tight hug and twirled her around.

"I can't thank you enough! The insurance companies will stop blocking me from working, thanks to you!"

Once he set her down, she smiled back, feeling the weight of the victory. "We'll stay one step ahead. But after this, anything else will look like sour grapes."

She shut off the projector and returned to her desk, mentally preparing for her next challenge.

"I have a flight to catch to Denver," she said, glancing at her assistant. "But when I get back, it's me, you, and Rachel, out on the town. I owe you both."

Her assistant smiled. "By the bounce in his step, I think it's safe to say things went well. Oh, and you have a call."

Jessica grabbed the phone. "Jessica Hartford."

"Ms. Hartford, this is Kimberly Ridder from Bluegrass Records," came the soft Southern voice on the other end.

Jessica sat up straight, the hairs on the back of her neck prickling. "What can I do for you, Ms. Ridder?"

"Kimberly, please. I need the best publicist this side of the Mason-Dixon."

Jessica's mind raced. The last thing she expected was a call from Bluegrass Records. "Well, you've got her. I'm the best you'll find."

"Which is why I'm calling," Kimberly replied, her voice laced with dry humor. "Everyone else has quit on me. You're my last resort."

Jessica smiled to herself, feeling the familiar rush of competition stir in her veins. She was ready for this.

Coming June 2025

www.ingramcontent.com/pod-product-compliance
Lightning Source LLC
LaVergne TN
LVHW040954150826
845672LV00002B/692

* 9 7 9 8 2 3 0 5 7 3 6 9 2 *